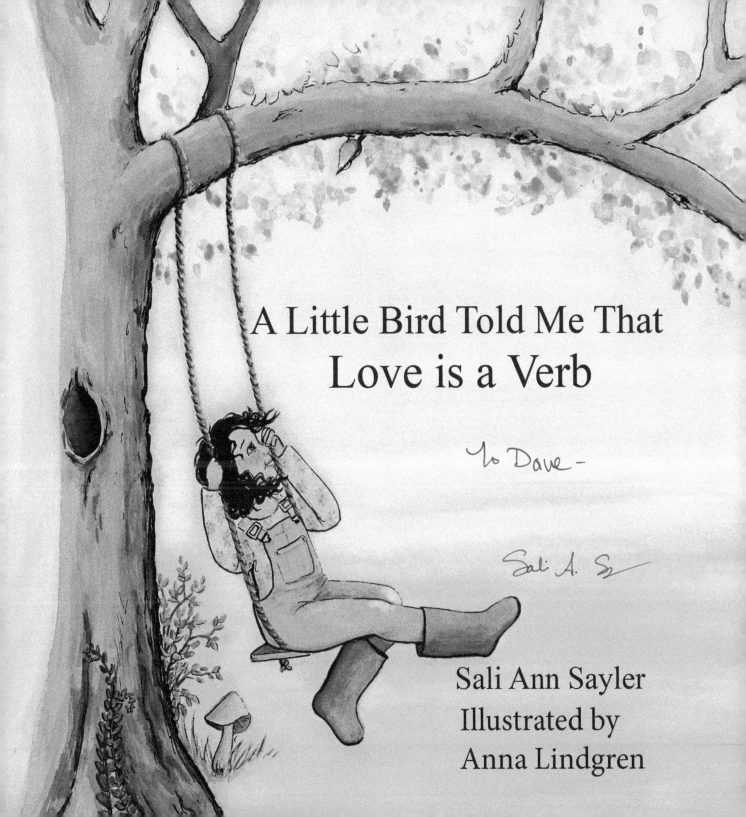

A Little Bird Told Me That Love is a Verb

To Dave –

Sali A. S

Sali Ann Sayler
Illustrated by
Anna Lindgren

Visit our website at www.whitebirdpublications.com

ISBN: 978-1-63363-310-0
LCCN: 2019933694

For Blaine, for being my one and only birding buddy.
For Ella and Alyssa, for bringing magic into the world and joy into my life.
And for Brian, for being my best friend and biggest fan.

-Sali Ann Sayler

To Quincy, Maysa, Brooklyn, Macy and Chandler in sweet memory of our adventures and fairy houses.
To my soulmate Luke and to Gerald Magnus who during the illustrating of this book came into this world and made me a mother. You are my treasures.

-Anna Lindgren

My house is full, from the bottom to the top. I have a lil' sis, a big bro, a mom, and a pop.

We also have fur friends and sometimes Aunt Sue. She visits in summer and at holidays, too.

Some days we get along, and "I love you" fills the air.

But other days the air is filled with "Mine!"—"Get out!"—
"No fair!"

When my full house gets loud, and I'm feeling unheard, I walk through the forest and talk to the birds. I talk to the robins and the little chickadees. I talk to the flickers, and they talk to me.

On just such a day, not long ago, I met a young nuthatch who was flying real low.

She sat on a tree trunk, upside down as they do, and sang me a song from morning till noon.

That little bird told me that love is a verb. She tweeted it sweetly, and here's every word.

She sang, "A verb is an action like dance, jump, or play. Love is a verb, not just something that you say. Love is an action like a wink or a smile. The smallest of gestures can last a long while."

That little nuthatch was one smart little bird. I felt my heart growing with every word.

She chirped, "Put your feelings in motion with a card or a letter. Knowing you're loved makes every day better. Love can't be measured with rulers or pie charts. Love is infinite when it comes from your heart."

They say owls are wise, and magpies and crows, but that red-breasted nuthatch is the smartest I know.

She trumpeted, (for effect) "Love can be loud," (then quietly) "or the softest of whispers. Love should be shared between brothers and sisters. Sharing is easy; even babies can do it. When you give love, you get love; that's all there is to it."

I thanked that nuthatch for a lesson well learned. Then I ran home to my family for a love fest well earned.

I hugged my mom, my pop, and my goofy Aunt Sue. I kissed my big brother who shouted out, "Ew."

I brushed the dog and then scratched the cat's ears.

I tickled my baby sis till we both were in tears.

Love is a verb; you can do it every day, with your actions and deeds and with every word you say.

Love is a verb! How do you put love into action?

I show my family love by…

I show my friends love by…

I show my school love by…

I show my neighborhood love by…

I show my community love by…

I show the earth love by…

Share your ideas of how to put love into action at:

saliannsayler.com.

CPSIA information can be obtained
at www.ICGtesting.com
Printed in the USA
LVHW070020090319
610019LV00002B/3/P